Praise for RUNAWAYS and MICHAEL J. SEIDLINGER

"This smart story ought to prompt readers to second-guess the impulse to write—or to tweet."   *—Publishers Weekly*

"Michael J. Seidlinger has written a weird and beautiful and slightly deranged meditation on the horror show that is the writer's life in the age of social media. Think Samuel Beckett's *Stories & Texts for Nothing* only here it's tweets, retweets, quote tweets, DM's and the special hell of 'going viral.' I can't tell you how many times I burst out laughing in horror and recognition at the darkly funny and depraved state of our protagonist 'a writer.' Finally a book that takes the craft of not writing as seriously as the craft of writing. Seidlinger is a literary iconoclast who fills the page with riotous and heartbreaking truths about how we live now: cerebral, punk rock, stylish, and sensitive."

— Gabe Hudson, author of *Gork, the Teenage Dragon*

"Part tale and part literary Twitter discourse, Seidlinger delivers a humorous and incisive look into the life and neuroses of the modern writer. *Runaways* wormed under my skin in the best of ways, invoking bad habits, sage advice, and all of the stories writers tell themselves when faced with a blank page. Required reading for any writer looking to feel less alone in the trenches."

— Sequoia Nagamatsu, author of *How High We Go in the Dark* and *Where We Go When All We Were Is Gone*

"A portrait of the writer as a procrastinator, professional self-doubter, caffeine connoisseur, and social-media addict, *Runaways* wallows in the manifold frustrations of this extravagantly frustrating process—yet it ultimately left this fellow sufferer feeling optimistic and ready to confront the blank page once more."

—Mason Currey, author of *Daily Rituals: How Artists Work*

"Whether it's craft or memoir, I'm constantly buying books on writing. This one will be on my desk as a touchstone to be read everyday for my mental health. It's essential. It's a writer's heart's song, capturing the true agony and ecstasy of being an artist today. *Runaways* is the book for every writer and everyone who wants to understand

—Jimin Han, a

D1208113

Additional Praise for MICHAEL J. SEIDLINGER

"Seidlinger holds a mirror to the contemporary writer, a narcissist and addict with often little to say. Deft, gracefully slender, and deeply upsetting: *Runaways: A Writer's Dilemma* is a plea to every artist to throw their phone into a river."

—Christopher Zeischegg, author of *The Magician*

"Michael Seidlinger writes beautifully, with purpose, with skill."
—Bud Smith, author of *Teenager*

"Seidlinger captures the doubt, desperation, and deceit involved in finding purpose. Ultimately, is this "purpose" of our own making, or is it a prescribed notion to become someone manifested by and for others? *Dreams of Being* captures the relatable fear in being who we are, complexity and all."   —Jennifer Baker, editor of *Everyday People: The Color of Life*

"I never trust people who use a middle initial, but Michael J Seidlinger is different. When I read his writing, I'm on my back, I'm having my behavior corrected: It's teaching me a lesson. And I can see stars."
—Scott McClanahan, author of *The Sarah Book*

"Michael J Seidlinger understands the messy mysterious business of being human, and of also looking to be wanted, needed, and validated."
—Ron Currie, author of *The One-Eyed Man*

"*Dreams of Being* is a fever dream, a religious text, a writer's notebook, a case of mistaken identity, a love letter. Jiro is one of the most fascinating characters you will ever read, and this is Michael Seidlinger at his very best, his sentences full of his particular energy and verve."
—Matthew Salesses, author of *Disappear Doppelgänger Disappear*

"Seidlinger continues his quest to become a literary chameleon, diving into new genres and remixing them into something wholly his own. His is a kingdom without borders."   —Joshua Mohr, author of *Model Citizen*

RUNAWAYS

A WRITER'S DILEMMA

MICHAEL J. SEIDLINGER

Future Tense Books

Portland, Oregon

RUNAWAYS: A WRITER'S DILEMMA

Paperback ISBN: 978-1-892061-89-8

Edited by Kevin Sampsell and Emma Alden.
Layout by Michael Kazepis.
Cover design by Alban Fischer.

First edition. Printed in the United States of America.

Published by Future Tense Books.
www.futuretensebooks.com
Portland, Oregon

—

Runaway—

(n) An idea, story, or mood that escapes the moment you are right in the middle of experiencing it.

A WRITER, A LITTLE BIT LONELY and a whole lot desperate, signed into social media. They didn't know what they were looking for. That was kind of the problem. They were having trouble getting started. They needed an idea, something that got them excited, but the point was they were still looking. They looked at a blank page. They looked for someone, anyone, to confirm what they felt was true. Was writing even worth the effort? They wanted to know there were others feeling the same pangs of disbelief and despair.

Just 1000 words today, that's all. A thousand words. Instead, they drafted a post.

The rest, you could say, was procrastination.

Everyone was busy writing, posting, posting about writing. It was overwhelming before it became encouraging. The idea could be a single screen-scroll away. A writer just needed to keep scrolling. Soon they found a post where someone talked about their favorite books. They talked about how a favorite book could change a person's life, more so how a favorite book could change multiple times over the course of a person's life. They were amazed by the beauty of the book, only to recognize that they had grown out of the book. Some commented about how their favorite books became touchstones as they grew as people, readers, and writers; others commented in agreement, how the books that blew them away years ago no longer carried the same effect. A writer lurked through the thread, eager to reply, yet stopped short of doing so. Something about it, hitting reply, seeing their thoughts among everyone else's, it was almost too much. So they didn't reply, instead moving on with the day, eventually googling different topics, things they had always found fascinating, in search of the elusive eureka a writer needed, the spark that led to *the* idea.

Hours later, after lunch and indulging in a few text message conversations with friends–pure distraction–a writer went back to research, only to find themselves drifting back to social media. While there, they checked the same thread, noting that the number of comments, likes, and shares had escalated threefold. It made them feel left out, even though they didn't know anyone in the conversation, much less the writer of the original post.

Still, the eagerness to write or say *something* returned, and soon they were laboring over a post of their own. The last time they posted? They couldn't remember. Too long, not long enough. A writer thought about the right words to describe that feeling of being overcome with the glow of a good book.

The envy and desire of having been the writer that wrote it. That feeling was euphoria.

The three stages of book euphoria ✪:
🙂 I love this book
🙁 I hate this book
😳 I am this book

The moment it became a post, a writer's focus was how well the post did. Refresh, check, refresh: A writer watched as it got a few likes, not much else.

A stranger replied, "Too real." And that was that. No further engagement.

Back to Google for some research. A writer continued until a topic presented itself. It wasn't quite excitement. Not at first. They didn't realize they had an idea. Instead, they were too busy thinking about not having much of a following. Maybe they'd come up with another post, something about doing book research, but nothing really came to mind.

Drawing a blank, a writer returned to reading.

Not much time passed before a writer was once again distracted. This time it was a call from their brother. Shit, they thought. Not now. Still, a writer knew they'd feel guilty if they didn't answer, so for the remainder of the hour, they listened to their brother chat about how well he was doing. Money made, new promotions: an all-around success story. Eventually, the conversation wound its way back to a writer's current predicament. A writer reacted defensively, "I want to be a writer." The brother reacted, "Sure, take as much time as you need. Eventually you'll need to, you know, earn a living."

From there, the conversation reached a stalemate. There wasn't much else to be said, so their brother talked about himself a bit longer before ending the call with a single, decimating statement.

"I'm worried about you."

Running away from reality, a writer lost themselves in the day's discourse. They occasionally returned to their Word document full of random facts and figures, quotes and pictures: research for a book. When a writer was overwhelmed, they often froze up, making no further progress on a project. And that was exactly what happened until a writer returned to a passage, one in particular, and while reading, the idea expanded enough to snap a writer into full attention.

Wait. . . a writer mused about the possibilities.

Could it? Isolating the passage, writing down some notes. There it was: the idea. *This could be it.* A writer could be so excitable sometimes. The first sentence didn't always need to be difficult. The words appeared on screen, one after the other, so effortlessly a writer almost didn't realize an afternoon became evening and one page became three. When they came up for air, they found whole paragraphs written along with the euphoria that made a writer think, *Maybe I can really do this.*

Who could they tell? A good question.

They went online and contemplated how to translate their feelings.

Nothing like a good first sentence. Sets the tone. It takes your breath away. It makes you incredibly envious of the book you're holding, wishing you had written such a masterful sentence.

Perhaps a little eager, but a writer just got an idea, and best of all: It was something they really wanted to write about! So what if it comes off as too earnest and borderline unbearable? In that moment, their post received a few shares, a few words of encouragement. All the validation a writer needed to live in for the hour, maybe the evening.

When a writer returned to the idea, the excitement—*though still present*—had changed, and whatever momentum they had moments ago had somehow waned.

Was it worth worrying about?

A writer gave it some thought and then decided they had done well enough for the day. And no, they did not hit that 1000-word quota that day, or the day after that. But soon, perhaps, a writer would begin filling page after page full of words.

A western gunfight standoff but it's me staring at my laptop *fingertips hesitating over the keyboard* and my laptop staring at me *blank Word doc cursor blinking*

It wasn't going so well. A writer dedicated an entire weekend to start the novel. When Friday night rolled around, the anxiety about tomorrow's big day led them to having "one too many." They hadn't been drinking lately, which lowered their tolerance. A writer knew better than to drown themselves in alcohol, but they were equal parts ecstatic and anxious. Mix in a few friends with no intention other than to get shit-faced to celebrate the end of yet another work week, you bet a writer regretted the headache come Saturday morning.

The meds and water and instant ramen didn't kick in and kill off the hangover until mid-afternoon. At that point, a writer had already begun nursing new worries.

```
*sits down to write*
my brain: don't say it
don't say it
don't say it
don't say it
don't say it
don't say it
don't say it
don't say it
don't say it
don't say it
don't say it
don't say it
don't say it
don't say it
me: "Think I'll check social media."
```

Before a writer could see how the post was received, they returned to their work-in-progress. What happened to the euphoria? The idea was still there; a writer had the notes, the outline, and even the stack of reference books to prove it. But something was still missing. The mood, the feel, the spark that came from that day, that initial idea, was gone.

It ran away.

A runaway.

All that was left for a writer was an entire weekend stretching out in front of them, and the increasingly dire need to get the words down. It was too easy to lose momentum, becoming distracted by email, the ceaseless stream of news, streaming video, the compulsion to step away for a second and grab a bite, maybe another cup of coffee. The itch was there, the tensing of their muscles and nerves with every half-thought and gesture luring them away from their work-in-progress. A writer watched nearly an hour of news clips, scrolled aimlessly through their watchlist only to settle on watching nothing. They debated whether they should order delivery. It had been a while since they had a burger from their favorite fast-food chain. More like a week. Instead, a writer reached for some of the reference books. They flipped through countless pages, reading in hopes they would figure out how a writer could come up with such impossible, downright masterful narratives.

Sometimes I just need a book right next to me—no intention of reading it, or picking it up, just the occasional glance—and suddenly my mood is lifted.

A writer turned away from social media, denying the distraction because they were already so beyond distracted. They hadn't noticed yet, but they were already chasing after the runaway, trying to regain the energy to write.

It was the first day, the first *real* day on the work-in-progress, and in about an hour, it would soon become night. Scaring themselves straight, a writer got to work. Once they managed to get started, they kept writing, unsure of where they were taking the story, but also reluctant to stop. A writer couldn't stop now. They didn't notice how much time had passed until they started feeling it in their neck, and then their fingers; the tension of a body that had been frozen into place for hours.

A writer looked and discovered their word count had exceeded 1000 words. But they wouldn't dare read what they wrote. A writer didn't want to tempt being self-critical this early in the work. So they signed in and posted what was on their mind. . .

The writing process:
1) Idea
2) Research
3) Start writing
4) Keep writing
5) Lose your shit
6) Regain your shit
7) Edit and revise
8) Editing
9) More editing
10) Submit
11) Shit gets rejected
12) Keep submitting
13) Turns out someone likes your shit
14) Shit gets published

A writer could so easily worry about what was yet to come—the subsequent drafts, high possibility of rejection—but instead they relished in the positive responses, the fact that the post had done well, a large number of shares, the interest and attention of what was such an easy and effortless post lasting late into the night.

In the morning, still high off a well-received post, a writer posted again.

 Writing constraint: For every sip of coffee, write two sentences.
See how many sentences you can get down before a) the coffee turns cold or b) you're all jittery opening browser tabs by the dozen.

They tried their own constraint. A fresh cup of coffee, they wrote two sentences. A sip and another two. The caffeine high snuck up on them, the jitters and panic sending them back into social media. They wrote exactly two pages before they could no longer focus. It was a Sunday, the last eight hours of their inaugural, self-imposed writing lockdown. It was almost over.

They needed, needed, *needed*, to hit 5,000 words. A writer knew it probably wouldn't happen, so they began rereading the day's sentences, laboring over word-choice and the cadence of the prose. The more they fixated, the worse it sounded.
None of what they had written made any sense.

This needs so much work, a writer thought.

 I'm not a writer: I just spend an inexorable amount of time figuring out if "inexorable" fits best in this sentence.

Oh, how quickly things fade. The post got three likes. A writer deleted the post and went back to editing their work. They stopped drinking coffee and eventually the jitters stopped. Still, the high brought with it the low. A writer started to get tired and thought about a nap. *Just an hour, tops.* They yawned, scrolled through their newsfeed for 10 minutes before their eyelids went heavy. A writer stood from their seat and stumbled to bed.

When they woke up, the sun had begun to set.

The work week kicked in and soon the distance between the next writing session and the last lengthened to eight days. On a Tuesday morning, a writer woke up early to write. Two hours seemed like a good enough amount of time. They hadn't accounted for the sluggishness that often resulted with waking early when a person wasn't used to it. Dawn had not yet arrived.

A writer turned to the handful of craft books they owned, reading about writers talking about writing like it was a conquerable, completely possible act; you just needed to see it the way *they* saw it. Eventually, a writer abandoned the books and went back online.

They searched for popular writers like Margaret Atwood, Ursula K. Le Guin, and Toni Morrison.

 Your first name + your last name = your struggling writer name.

A writer posted about their feelings, and what did they get in return? Their first viral post, a complete disruption of their work-in-progress. Between the steady notifications to the looming possibility of someone messaging them, a writer enjoyed the dopamine rush of being part of the social media spotlight, effectively their "15 seconds of fame." Soon they would have to go to work. Throughout the day, they'd be distracted by notifications, the post periodically shared by users with verified accounts, hundreds of thousands of followers, whole careers built around a performative brand. Their name meant something. A writer envied it all but had already lost any sense of appreciation for their post. Following the rush, they experienced withdrawal, the desperate urge to replicate and follow-up one viral post with another. There would be no writing done today.

When it was all said and done, the post had hit 18k shares with a high six figures of likes. By then, Tuesday had rolled over to Friday and a writer's weekend was too busy to get any writing done. They had already felt disconnected from their work-in-progress, the idea and all that had gotten them excited. . . it was more than a runaway.

Losing that sense of momentum, every word of their work-in-progress felt lifeless. Every sentence brought them one step closer to admitting that they did not know where to go next. It felt like a failure.

During a dull moment in the workday, a writer tried something different. Instead of taking advice from writers about how to fight through the uncertainty and despair, they opted to peruse book recommendations and whole articles about finding your next good read. The voracious readers were so enthusiastic about books, it could make a writer envious.

There was a whole world where avid readers chatted about searching for rare editions, curating their own library of books, going as far as designing their own book covers.

It was enough to encourage a writer, almost.

Reading - the act of escaping into the despair of another to pretend your despair will somehow be forgotten when you finish reading.

Think about how many books an avid reader reads in a given year. A writer vaguely recalled a time when their association with the book was purely enjoyment and escapism. Long before they chased writerly ambitions, a writer was a reader that bought a book a day, sometimes two. They couldn't get enough, and every new book felt like a life-altering experience. A writer dabbled in nostalgia, trying to remember when they made the switch. When did they begin to pursue writing? What made an avid reader any different than being someone who eventually tried their hand at writing a book of their own?

Writing - the act of filling pages with despair in hopes that someone else will find solace in comparing their despair with yours.

The more a writer read about someone else's reading habits, the more they wanted to read about the act of reading. Between saving articles to read later, they noticed the Word document still open on their desktop. Seeing it made them feel sad.

They had a new post in no time.

 "Will I ever be able to write again?" Said every writer after a bad writing session.

If only it was this easy to actually write. A writer found it increasingly easier to be active and successful on social media the worse they felt about their own craft.

Could that feeling run away from them too? The thought of it simply too much, a writer returned to their blood-sucking job. On the commute home from work, they started adding books to their wish-list, thinking about all the writers who managed to finish *and publish* their books so that people could add them to their TBR stacks.

A writer focused on one book in particular, reading the author's bio, going to the author's website, the author's Wikipedia page, reading up on the author's life.

When they reached the author's account, they discovered that the author hadn't posted in over a year. It made them feel a certain way, as though a writer maybe didn't need to "take part" in public discourse to service their platform and careers, but before they could comprehend the totality of the discovery, that feeling ran away too.

 When feeling low, my immediate reaction is to hype-up/help-out another writer, if only so that—at that very moment—we both don't feel forgotten.

It was the best a writer could do—post about being depressed.
Looking at the wish-list, the hundreds of titles they had added,
a writer understood the sheer impossibility of writing a book.

 Writing a book is like looking both ways
before you cross the street and then
falling into a pit that descends to hell.

People seemed to enjoy the post, so much that it gained
hundreds of likes, but a writer felt the validation, the euphoria,
the dopamine rush, run away from them right when it should
have been its strongest.

Immediately after a writer returned home from a long
day at the day-job, they sat at their desk, tempting some sort
of recovery. Maybe they could take whatever this idea was
supposed to be and follow the trail it left behind. Maybe a
writer could still turn it around.

Then they got a text from their ex, wasting the energy they
might have had. After reaching the point of the conversation
where their ex would clearly continue chatting until they were
exhausted, a writer set their phone aside and walked into the
kitchen.

Eating leftovers while streaming a new show, in the back
of a writer's mind was always the wonder of how a show was
written—who wrote it, how did they manage such a seemingly
impossible feat? What about the writers who were famous for
being on social media, with their massive legion of followers,
everything they post trending no matter how obvious or
inane—did it amount to a book deal, a new opportunity? Did

social media correlate with tangible success, or was it more of a performance of extensive social capital? After eating, a writer returned to their desk. Feeling the full weight of just how impossible it had quickly become, writing anything, they posted again, only distantly aware of how well the previous post did.

 The most difficult part of writing is–I cannot emphasize this enough–the writing.

A writer could have started over or they could have gone back and tried to iron out the problems. Of the two choices, they chose the latter, and on a lazy Sunday, they found the pieces that were once missing, the very details they couldn't figure out, the source of the impossibility.

Suddenly everything seemed like a great idea, and they couldn't stop brainstorming new characters, scenes, and chapters. A writer could almost get lost in the excitement, but then they ended up checking social media.

Being a writer:

 Pros) You can write anything you want. Cons) You can't write anything you want.

An hour passed quickly while a writer clicked and scrolled and replied to every notification. Sunday morning became a bright Sunday afternoon; a writer was shocked to see how elusive time truly was. They signed out and got back to their work-in-progress.

A new constraint: They wouldn't check social media until they wrote one page.

Soon it was amended to be three paragraphs, and eventually a writer settled on one paragraph per every glance online.

How long though?

They worried that if they were online for any longer than 10 minutes, they might never return to their work. So that's how the 10-minute time limit started. A writer denied any invitations to hang out later, knowing well that they shouldn't be so quick to run away from the very thing that ran away from them earlier that month. It was difficult to turn people down, especially their close friends, and even the person they wanted to date. But a writer declined to make plans. They called it discipline. A writer began to understand which sacrifices they were willing to make, even if they worried about what they might miss while taking the time.

> The only excuse you'll ever need -
> "Hey, you going to the party tonight?"
> Sorry, I'm writing.
> "Hey, you have that first draft yet?"
> Sorry, I'm writing.
> "Hey, you mail the rent check yet?"
> Sorry, I'm writing.

The afternoon was productive. By the time a writer had reached a thousand words, it wasn't yet 3:00PM. A writer was so motivated, they continued writing. From the page to social media to page, a writer finished writing a new chapter. They took a quick break for dinner, and then found themselves right back to work, plotting out the next chapter. With every new idea, a writer could not believe just how exciting and magical writing could be.

This is why *people write*, they thought.

Just as quickly, they found themselves looking at the immensity of the work-in-progress, so many words, so much editing, and so many drafts. It was overwhelming, but they were in it, finally right in the middle of it. And they enjoyed every part of it, no matter how vulnerable it made them feel. At least there would be no more runaways.

They were determined to stick with it.

 As writers, and more so as artists, we set ourselves up for failure. We must if we dare to achieve anything.

Months of constant routine work, only going out once or twice a week, and they had the draft. . . **RIGHT THERE**. In a simple, unassuming file-folder, a Word document, the culmination of eight months of work. They grabbed a bottle of whiskey and had Word run all the usual stats, number of lines, unique characters, time spent on this project—every single detail. Just because.

They poured themselves a glass and thought about who to share the news with. But everyone they knew probably wouldn't care, or rather they would at least pretend to care, and would gladly share in the celebration. But who would *actually* understand what this felt like, without discounting it?

A writer turned to social media.

They tried writing an announcement, but after a few attempts, they could already feel the euphoria fading and panicked. They took another sip of whiskey and decided not to post.

A writer could almost feel the draw of the discourse. When they were online, they could feel the anxiety of not being able to keep up; when offline, they battled the ever-present feeling of missing out. They loved being online. They hated being online. The initial draw—that feeling of being able to connect with others, especially the writing community—had lapsed after initially investing themselves into being active online. Nowadays, a writer found themselves cross-checking every thought and feeling with an ever-present question: "Is it worth posting on social media?" Fishing for likes and validation, they fell into a dependent relationship with a platform that could easily pass them over. A writer forgot the moment they no longer *wrote* stories and started *posting* content.

Ursula K. Le Guin's writing routine is the ideal writing routine.

5:30AM—wake up and lie there and think.
6:15AM—get up and eat breakfast (lots).
7:15AM—get to work writing, writing, writing.
Noon—lunch.
1-3PM—reading, music. (1/2)

3-5PM—correspondence, maybe house cleaning.
5-8PM—make dinner and eat it.
After 8PM—I tend to be very stupid and we won't talk about this. (2/2)

It came off as wisdom, advice from a true legend. A writer was merely sharing it. It went viral and would continue to get picked up for months. Their most popular post. A writer never forgets what inspired a post, but the longer they tried to explain what compelled them to post Ursula K. Le Guin's admirable writing routine, the more they desired to keep their true reasons (to challenge themselves, to connect with readers, to prove to themselves that they can finish *and* publish a book) to themselves. A writer didn't want the euphoria to run away. They continued to post quite frequently throughout the week.

The writer, in percentages—
19.5% uncontrollable / unstable ego
28% should be reading / instead on social media
30% obsessively talking about writing
25% caffeine high / caffeine low
7% online shopping / online brooding
.5% actually writing

They took a Friday off and tried to write an essay detailing how they managed to finish writing their draft, but it quickly devolved into a series of posts, each received less warmly than the last.

Joan Didion kept her manuscripts in bed
James Joyce wrote in crayon
Agatha Christie ate apples in the tub
Haruki Murakami runs a shit ton of miles
Flannery O'Connor kept a zoo of animals
I'm watching YouTube videos
You're on social media
Everyone has their writing process

A writing process never seemed real until a writer had taken it out for a spin, tried it on for size, and wrestled with the learning curve.

Daily writing quotas, complete with words of encouragement –

10 words – you got this.
100 words - you got this.
500 words - you got this.
1,000 words - you got this.
5,000 words - what are you, god?
10,000 words - if you love writing so much why don't you MARRY IT?

A writer found that they were more of a word-count type of writer, but the post got responses involving different methods of measuring progress. Some counted pages. Some aimed for a chapter; some worked from an outline, and some worked towards preconceived benchmarks.

Word counts for writers: a daily guilt:

Michael Crichton: 10,000 words
Anne Rice: 3,000 words
Maya Angelou: 2,500 words
Stephen King: 2,000 words
Mark Twain: 1,400 words
Holly Black: 1,000 words
J.G. Ballard: 1,000 words
Ian McEwan: 600 words
Me today: -71 words

The post had originated from a specific analysis of their Word stats and a two-hour deep dive on famous writers' word counts. Any google search with "famous writer" quickly generated an hour's worth of scrolling, reading, and parsing of an intense amount of content.

Imagine being Haruki Murakami, a full-time writer making enough income (and fame) from his creative writing that he doesn't need to do any publicity for his books. He can be as reclusive as he wants, living life in the rural area of Tokyo. And, of course, he has the time and clarity to maintain a healthy mental and physical lifestyle. That book about how he's a runner, it's essentially his entire writing process in book-form for other writers to marvel at and envy. Murakami wakes up every day with a physical drive to run and a mental urge to write weird books with talking cats and lonely men for his legion of fans.

Imagine being Stephen King. Every day you wake up knowing you are Stephen Motherfucking King, writer that can put anything on the page that will seemingly scare and satiate the masses. Every book turns into a movie; every book is a one-way ticket to more money. King wakes up with his typewriter in mind. Maybe King wakes up with an ironclad ego, walking into his office like he's stepping into the ring, about to go 12 rounds with his typewriter and he's the stud, the champion who can crush the typewriter like an aluminum can. King enters his office like some action hero, complete with a catchphrase. He points to the typewriter and says, "I will use you, I will write you, and I will finish you." Every day King sits down and writes a novel.

Imagine being Margaret Atwood. Years of putting in the work, and now a book you wrote back in the 1980s finally gets adapted and becomes a mega-hit among viewers. Now you wake up every morning with an inbox overflowing with fan letters and curiosities, many of them barely even recognizing those years of struggle and rejection. Hell, most of them barely even acknowledge your extensive bibliography or that you are a writer. Imagine what it feels like to receive correspondence from media outlets, universities, and publishers begging for a profile, a prestigious keynote, and even a sequel to that book you wrote so long ago. Imagine what that feels like. To be there, staring back at you is the opposite of the void. Without a doubt, when all is said and done, and you leave behind this life, you will never be forgotten.

Imagine being a financially successful writer, who can use those dollar signs to build a life (and process) that has as much space as it needs to remain inspired. The understanding that you have enough fans to attract publishers to your newest writing, long before anyone knows anything about the story, well. . . a writer might never fully know what that feels like. Imagine, though—a book garners a seven-figure advance *and* it sells well.

Must be nice.

Inspiration on an installment plan:

1) Write love letters to your favorite books.
2) Crush on your favorite poems.
3) Memorize your favorite lines and recite them whenever you're feeling blocked.

It was inspiring to see what such great literary thinkers were able to achieve. It was the kind of thing that made a writer daydream. But before they could enjoy the daydream, it ran away and left them feeling empty, with thoughts like:

What about me? Will anyone ever google search my name looking for insight into my process?

Why doubt that story idea you have when ones like "young hetero couple face tragedy, fall in epic love, live in North Carolina" have fueled Nicholas Sparks' entire career?

They got a little snarky in response, posting something that was essentially a reaction to a much more popular user's post about *The Shape of Water*, a controversial film, one that was being charged with claims of plagiarism. A writer couldn't focus on the vitriol spreading online about the film. Instead they posted again.

 The book you're writing today isn't the book you'll be writing tomorrow.

Eventually, the first draft had faded from their mind. A writer hadn't yet understood that they still had a mountain of work to do on it. It was, after all, a first draft.

 Why is it that the stories we haven't written always seem more interesting than the ones we write?

They mused about the fleetingness of any positive feeling, especially with one's writing. It is so powerful at its onset, yet by the time a writer could put it into words, it became a failed, useless incomplete thing. A writer finally accepted that euphoria would always run away from them; they held on, hoping it would last a little bit longer. Feeling a little lonely, a writer tried something else.

 Motivational prompts for Tuesday
Read some fucking poems!
Write a fucking poem!
Read a goddamn story!
Write a goddamn story!
Read more of that book!
Write more of that book!

Almost immediately, they lost 11 followers. There was no direct correlation to their latest post; it might have been the fact that they had posted a dozen times about the same subject in the span of a day. Who really knew? And it didn't matter; a writer became emotional, feeling disillusioned and hurt. It was baffling to see it happen. It triggered all sorts of worried and frayed thoughts—screen-capped posts shared on anonymous message-boards, people scrolling and seeing their profile picture and getting an emotional response, and not a good one. *Get that nonsense off my timeline.* And another worry—what if their followers were getting tired of them, no longer interested, the luster of first impressions lost? Is a follower the same as a fan?

For every high, they reached a deeper low.

 The first draft begins with a draft and ends with starting the fuck over.

After a short break (read: months), a writer returned to their draft with newfound determination. They began by rereading every sentence, being as objective and stern with their edits as possible. Almost as soon as they began, barely making it into chapter two, they stalled out and became distracted.

 Do you remember what it was like before you felt the pressure to write all the time?

A writer remembered what it had used to feel like—back when the blank page was nothing more than an escape, a chance to fill it with an adventure written purely for *fun*, and for no one else but themselves. Whole Word documents had existed, upwards of a hundred pages of words, an outpour with sustained enthusiasm, and then. . . well that was it. There was this sense of joy and intrigue in all that writing, a writer's "early writing," they figured it was called. Before they compared their writing to others, began studying and exploring the craft in the framework of being a writer, donning that title, the title beginning to inform how they viewed themselves and interacted with others. Before all that noise, a writer thought purely about being "me" or "myself" and the act of writing not as "writing," but pure and simple writing. They chased such thoughts, distantly hoping they might return to that space, if only for a little while. But soon they would have to snap back to reality, the expectant screen staring back.

When the editing went well, they could see the sentences making more sense, what the beauty of a turn-of-phrase could do when given the time to gestate, but just as soon as editing could really show it's true power, it stabbed a writer in the back with another confusing sentence, a plot hole, an entire section of the book that simply didn't work.

Continually shifting between "I love this," and "I hate this," regarding writing forever until the end of time.

It made a writer feel like they weren't, in fact, a writer. They wondered if they were just fooling themselves. The more they scrolled and saw other writers doing so well, being published in highly prestigious publications and getting books out there *(Bestseller! Constantly on various best-of lists! Unrelenting images and video of the book on people's shelves!)*, the more they felt inferior.

They edited a few lines, but their heart wasn't in it.

A writer thought about what their writing routine might be if they didn't have social media and other digital distractions knocking them down, continually capturing their eye.

They sat down with a piece of paper and a pen. Denying the use of a keyboard, they wrote in longhand what such a routine might be. Something with a typewriter perhaps, or perhaps exclusively the tactile feel of the pen and ink marking the page.

They would still have the routines before the session: the settling in feeling, the sipping of coffee or tea and the sitting, the act of slowing down movement to save it for mental motions. Music. A writer would desire music, no matter if there was a computer involved. Records would do just fine, and maybe even better. Pictures pinned to the walls instead of a file folder of saved images from the internet. Maybe more exercise than they usually got—longer walks and more frequent runs. Their routine would likely deal less in doubt without the distraction, to be reminded of what they were not, and might never be.

The page filled, they read it back aloud and then, in the calmness of the current moment, exhaled deeply and tore the paper to pieces.

The writer's anthem:

This coffee will help me write.
This nap will help me write.
This wine will help me write.
This pizza will help me write.
Buying this jacket will help me write.
This post will help me write.
Binge-streaming an entire show will help me write.

Other users added their own helpful hints, most taking the humor in stride, but a writer quickly lost interest. It was almost like the more attention they got, the more they wanted to push back, run away from the positive feeling. They wondered why, not quite able to grasp that the real reason was due to past abandonments. Opening up to someone ultimately pushed them away, seeing their interest fade and go by the wayside. A writer learned to cut out the middle, jumping to the conclusion: They keep their guard up, never letting most in.

A writer guarded against future runaways.

Two ways to make a writer smile—
1-Tell them you read their work.
2-Tell them you "plan on" buying their book. (1/2)

Two ways to make a writer cry—
1-Tell them you read their work.
2-Tell them you "plan on" buying their
book. (2/2)

A writer watched as one like became 12 likes, zero shares became a dozen. The post would do well, but what about a writer's mental health? The editing was wearing thin.

All they could think or post about was reading.

When someone borrows a book, they're basically saying, "Hey, this book's mine now."

A writer had so much to say about this topic. Clearly, other writers did too. The thread was long enough to perhaps fill a book, and yet a writer continued chiming in. A writer felt compelled to like and answer every comment. Distantly, they wondered if doing so somehow devalued their opinion. After a few replies, they became fully involved in the debate.

Do you ever need to hold onto a specific book? Do you ever give it away only to be surprised by how easily it was, forgetting that you had owned it? A writer mulled over such thoughts, the debate fueling such meditations. Is a book like part of someone's brain? If you get rid of a book, is the space its absence creates worth more than the book?

They noticed that one writer replied and then never returned, not even after someone tagged them in a response. A writer that didn't like comments, especially those that directly engage with their own content, seemed enigmatic and elusive; it felt like leaving them unanswered made them more interesting, borderline "bad boy" behavior. It's like the saying "Don't read the comments." People want what they can't have, especially the attention of someone who doesn't give it so easily. You want the attention of those that seldom gave it.

> The thing about reading is there's so much more to read.
> The thing about writing is you never write enough.

In the back of a writer's mind, they desired the attention. This was always the case, the need for validation, a desire to make sure they weren't invisible.

Exes and literary agents.

Writers and editors.

A family member that takes their writing seriously.

Friends, new and old.

The literary community.

Any community.

Themselves.

> When you pick up a new book you (be honest)—
>
> a) Feel the texture of the cover.
> b) Open and smell the pages.
> c) Flip to first/last pages.
> d) Take a picture/selfie with it.
> e) Dream and fantasize about reading it.
> f) Immediately forget about it and buy another.

When that post didn't go over well–eight likes, nothing else–a writer became fully distracted with the pursuit of creating a post that stuck. They wouldn't let go of the task until they had one successful post for that day.

A writer was aware of their budding habit, craving the validation from others daily or they'd feel off-balance. They were already an addict, denying the severity of the dependence.

 The REAL reason they made hardcover books is so that when you fall asleep reading, they hit you in the face and you wake the fuck back up.

People laughed, the post getting some shares. It took a writer 10 seconds to come up with that one, while so many others labored over like a line in their book took hours. The posts that take the least amount of effort, much like the ones that aim for nothing other than to crack a joke always seem to do the best. A writer used the momentum to, once again, post a succession of content. Content? More like "content," because none of these posts amount to anything more than data on a server, demonstrations of validation and the dire need to take part in the "discourse."

Not content in the sense that a writer was adding to their work-in-progress; rather, "content" as a term used across social media to refer to posts, videos, and memes created by users to spread around, often in anticipation of gaining visibility and going viral. When a person chose to create content, they were adding to the "discourse" continuing to play out across social media. Little did a writer realize that the discourse, much like the creation of content, never really ends. Social media exists, and because it does, the discourse demands of its participants undivided attention.

What do we want?
TO DO ANYTHING ELSE.
When do we want it?
EVERY TIME WE SIT DOWN TO WRITE.

Them: What's it like writing a book?

Writer: Well, you get an idea, & you got notes, maybe. Then you type and then you delete. Revise and rethink. Then you do research and second guess your ability to write.

Them: Wow, okay then what?

Writer: Then you move to the next sentence.

Nobody:
Absolutely nobody:
Writer: "I shall write in just a second, don't you worry. But first I must have my coffee, my music, my notebook, and my writing jacket. I must also meditate about all those that have wronged me, and I'll settle in at my writing desk with books and..."

Me: Feeling good today. I should write.
Brain: Food.
Me: Ok, but then I'm going to write.
Brain: Social media.
Me: Fine, but then I'm writing.
Brain: What if you majored in finance?
Imagine how different your life could be.
You could have been successful.
Me: Dammit.

[reason why I forget to answer email]

-gets email
-hits reply
-types
-deletes
-types
-looks something up on Google
-checks social media
-gets angry
-looks at Wikipedia
-reads up on serial killers
-reads up on viruses
-dreams about the world ending
-forgets to write you back

Copying from someone else's viral post, a writer targeted their own inadequacies. They couldn't count them on one hand.

They ran through the usual, what first came to mind—*I'm anxious, lazy, neglectful, lonely, but want to be alone, but don't want to be alone, I don't know what I want, I have a lot of problems with control, I interrupt people and talk over people often, I see myself as a failure even though I often never give myself a shot, I seldom actually try, like **really** try, I don't work out*

*enough, I drink and eat too much, I spend money I don't have,
I'm in so much debt, I have no prospects, I'm alone and I am
starting to get used to being alone.*

Ironic, they thought. It was so much easier to list out their
flaws rather than their strengths. What of their strengths? *I. .
. like to read and write? I know a lot about movies? I can make a
mean omelet. . . yeah.*

What's the value of a "humble brag?" A writer understood
the term to be the act of veiling the good by being self-
deprecating to lessen the blow, fearing that being honest
might result in more unfollows. A writer tended to feel worse
when they came across another writer's humble brag. Being
vague made it easier to for the mind to wander, dredging up
all kinds of possibilities. And besides, most people could sniff
out a humble brag without any trouble.

> FANTASY -
> Wrote 1000 words
> Freelance invoices paid on time
> Pitched a handful of publications
> Edited two chapters of the novel
> Answered emails in a timely fashion
>
> REALITY -
> Just woke up from a 3-hour nap

Feeling restless, they closed the Word document. There would
be no editing today. They went for a walk, never looking up
from their phone. They checked their stats, compared their
online presence to other writers. A writer tempted developing
a nemesis, someone they envied so much they channeled all

hate into a one-sided relationship. Eventually, in a panic, a need for interaction, they posted something from their drafts, a post from a different time, back when they were still writing their draft, not editing it.

Things you'll find writers will gladly do to avoid writing their book:

- Clean their house.
- Listen to all your problems (and then prob write about it).
- Alphabetize their books, food items, anything.
- Quit their job, apply for new job.
- Break up with their partner, friend, etc.

A writer missed writing. They hated editing. The incomplete task was a weight on their shoulders for weeks before they eventually caved in and broke their weekend plans and locked themselves in their apartment with enough food and water (and booze) to make real progress.

They swore they wouldn't touch the booze until they had edited 50 pages of their draft. A writer wouldn't repeat past mistakes. But who was a writer kidding but themselves? Friday night, they craved a margarita. All they had was whiskey. It would have to do. Five shots later, they were passed out on the couch, their phone slowly sliding off their chest.

Writes a thousand words: feels like a failure.
Edits a single paragraph: feels like a genius.

Saturday morning was a panicked rush. Shockingly they didn't have a hangover, but they still went through the preventative measures: vitamin C, something greasy, coffee, a late-morning nap before doing a quick workout. By 3PM, a writer began editing. They fought off the pressures of a self-imposed deadline.

> Amount of time it takes to do things:
>
> Eat a bagel - 10 minutes.
> Clean your apartment - 1-2 hours.
> Pay a bill - 1-3 minutes plus additional 30min to cry.
> Watch a movie - 2-3 hours.
> Write a book: 1 year, 1 lifetime, infinite tears.

> How to prepare for an editing session –
>
> 1) Set a goal.
> 2) Set a soundtrack.
> 4) Coffee, tea, slab of concrete (what?).
> 5) Word doc, Scrivener, YouTube (ugh).
> 6) Post something (dammit).
> 7) Check status of post 10x per hour.
> 8) Perform a spell.
> 9) Say a prayer.
> 10) Say anything.

By 4:30PM, they had made it through a dozen pages. A writer never felt so productive. They checked social media as a reward for being so productive, but closed the app before they could get sucked in.

> Three simple words can increase your productivity tenfold:
>
> Write a book BEFORE YOU'RE DEAD.
> Learn to cook BEFORE YOU'RE DEAD.
> Do laundry BEFORE YOU'RE DEAD.
> Mail that fucking letter BEFORE YOU'RE DEAD.

Perhaps a writer's biggest pressure, the most important deadline, was doing all they could before they die. Write as much as they could before reaching their last breath. Leave behind whatever they could leave behind but get as much done so that when they reached the final moment, their own concluding scene, they could feel okay about finally letting go.

What would a writer leave behind? Clothes, books, some electronics, sure. But what would they leave behind that really said, *I was here?* A writer tried to come up with a list of people that would miss them, should they suddenly no longer exist tomorrow. They could maybe gather a dozen, if they put in a few acquaintances online. They thought about their social media, email, and other online password-protected accounts and then went back to the list and thought about who among the dozen they could entrust with their passwords. Who would they trust to retrieve all the unfinished and unpublished stories, novels, and fragments that remained on a cloud server, hidden behind 2-factor verification? Almost instantly, their imposter syndrome chimed in, "Who would give a shit about all your unpublished writing, much less publish it?"

Writer's order of operations—

- Arrange writing space.
- Coffee, tea, whatever.
- Answer emails, check social media.
- Drum up potential blurbs.
- Write acknowledgments.
- Make big book tour and promotional plans.
- Plan out next couple books.
- Actually start writing the book.

A writer dreamt of the book their manuscript might one day become. They picked out a handful of seemingly successful writers and wrote out possible letters of gratitude.

Really though, a writer felt sad yet hopeful, most times. They didn't really know how else to feel. Sadness and hope seemed to be their strongest feelings–the ones that came with being an aspiring and ambitious writer. They dreamt of being able to complete something, willfully opening previously closed doors of the mind in search of something to write about. Little did they realize that by opening those doors, they were no longer shut, and with it the onslaught of feelings surged from those archived corners, uncontrollable and beyond a writer's frequent desire to silence them.

The editing process:
1. Editing
2. More editing
3. Keep editing
4. Step away
5. Go back fresh
6. Find and replace every adverb (1/2)

7. Change chapter titles, then change them back
8. Realize, hey this isn't that bad
9. Give it another edit
10. Damn you're exhausted
11. Give it one more pass
12. Time for someone else to edit (2/2)

The editing process was more baffling to a writer than the actual writing. It was a confusing, grueling act. In addition to being repetitive, editing felt like having a therapist tell you, in excruciating detail, everything that's wrong with you, but stopping short of giving you any real solutions. Worse, the therapist would give you homework, enough to last you a lifetime.

A writer needed a drink, knowing they were feeding into temptation, developing increasingly bad habits. It had more to do with drowning out the despair.

Their productivity plummeted with increasing intensity, like the sound of ice melting in an empty whiskey glass.

Write drunk, edit drunk, throw away your manuscript drunk, come up with a new novel idea drunk, hate on famous writers drunk, never get any writing done because, yup, drunk.

Monday morning. A writer woke up with a splitting headache, but they made it their penance to wake up and move forward with their day. They worked from home, taking every spare moment to return to their manuscript, making little edits, fighting back the headache with productivity.

Anatomy of revision:

First draft: It's not good enough.
Third draft: It's still not good enough.
Seventh draft: Getting better, I think?
Tenth draft: Maybe I'll give it some space, move on to something else for now.
First draft of next book: Shit, it's just not good enough.

The manuscript would probably never be "good enough," but a writer added to their calendar a revised deadline. Their first draft had become a second draft and now, they tempted the final draft. Would three drafts be enough?

They gave themselves two and a half weeks to figure it out. Two and a half weeks to see if the manuscript might be called a novel.

A writer hoped that their editorial determination wouldn't run away from them too.

Two and a half weeks went by in a flash. A writer's manuscript still needed work. A third draft was necessary. After a two-day period of mourning, truly overwhelmed by how much work was left to be done, a writer made the decision, a very important and potentially stupid decision.

They decided to temporarily disable their account.

A writer gave themselves four months to complete a new draft.

They added in another two on either end for the handful of friends that said they'd give their manuscript a read. It was highly possible they'd need to give it a fifth draft. But they didn't want to worry about that. Not yet.

So, they posted one last time.

 Every novel is a class in learning how to write.

They gave the post an afternoon, yet they were too distracted to engage with anyone looking to engage with them, particularly the usual assortment of reply guys. They started a new notebook, created a music playlist that—in full—would take 18 hours if played straight through. When they weren't working, they were still working—the manuscript became as close to life as was possible. Six months, a writer thought.

It would take them eight.

What did a writer do after they completed the impossible, a more than reasonably edited manuscript, the culmination of nearly three years of work? A novel.

They drew a blank. Publish it, of course, but how? Social media was full of possible leads, but where to even begin? So quickly they had come to an understanding with their craft, only to once again, feel their grip loosen.

A writer did what any writer did: They researched publishing houses, agents, and in their darkest most doubtful moments, they researched self-publishing options. They drew up elaborate Excel spreadsheets with various open calls, submission deadlines, and other details that could easily be lost. A writer became good at managing their next move: submission.

Person reading book: "Oh, I get it."
* turns page *
Narrator: "They did not get it."

After a month of research—including a few informational calls with editors and agents, after an anxiety induced sleepless night of watching videos on YouTube about best-practices on landing an agent, selling your book, the whole frightening process—on a Wednesday morning, bright and early, 7:30AM, a writer sent out their first query to an agent.

Almost immediately they knew they had made a mistake. Their query letter was too verbose, way too formal; they reread it aloud and it sounded like something someone had transcribed by a text-to-speech reader.

To help curtail the anxiety, they went ahead and prepped their first submission to an independent press they had long since admired. If they couldn't get an agent, they could try on their own to sell the manuscript to an independent publisher.

The secret to being productive is being too poor to do much of anything else.

Right after posting, they checked their social stats. They noticed they had lost 38 followers. Perhaps not the best time to check their voicemail, a writer listened to an angry friend's message, claiming they hadn't heard from them "in ages" and accused a writer of being a neglectful friend. Seems they had completely no-showed a hangout. They wanted to apologize but everything seemed suddenly so overwhelming.

A writer wanted very much for this feeling to run away from them too.

 How to lose friends and alienate people: start writing a book.

Over the next couple months, a writer took special care to never over-submit. No carpet-bombing agents and publishers. They ran down their spreadsheet, submitting, submitting, submitting. They started to fear the rejection, knowing from what they heard from others that rejections always showed up first.

One lonely night, having done something stupid—getting drunk and rereading their manuscript, the inebriation making it impossible to concentrate on the sentences—a writer came to the conclusion that it was all horrible. *Publishing was horrible.*

 A play-by-play of the submission process:

1. Carefully construct query, taking special care that your writing is in the best shape possible. and you submit within the required parameters and deadlines.
2. Then you wait.
3. And wait.
4. And wait…

A writer was more resilient than they would ever give themselves credit for. They climbed out of that dark place and got back to life's various demands. It became a ritual, every Thursday afternoon, during lunch hour, they would spend a half-hour submitting their manuscript and the other half-hour researching current agent and press wish-lists.

On a lazy Saturday afternoon, a writer got their first rejection.

It was from an agent. They did their best to read the email without crying. It wasn't a form letter—that was good—but phrases like "championing it" and "you deserve an agent" and "cheering you on from the sidelines" came off as borderline passive-aggressive.

The agent didn't like their query. That was the takeaway.

A writer scrolled through their spreadsheet, finding the agent's name and marking the appropriate box, "REJECTION."

Things in a writer's brain:
- Every rejection
- Every project they haven't finished
- Every person that's ever been mean to them (1/2)

Things not in a writer's brain:
- Self-esteem
- The password to basically everything
- Mental math (2/2)

The day wasn't yet over. A writer received two more rejections, as if the editors of both presses had heard that an agent didn't want the manuscript, so they no longer cared either.

The stink of rejection. . .

One editor simply said, "This isn't quite the right fit," and then ended the letter quickly, "wishing you the best of luck." A writer deleted the rejection, not even worth saving. The other editor went into some detail about how they didn't connect with the characters, thought the book had too many flashbacks, and was essentially too experimental for their publishing house.

A writer paused and blinked, understanding the irony. The publishing house was known for publishing dense, highly experimental texts. That was their bread and butter.

Writer gets acceptance: "I'm so thrilled!"
forgets 10 min later
Writer gets rejection: "I'm so mortified!"
laments and broods for a month/year/forever

People online related to rejection more than they did the act of writing. Every post involving rejection resulted in hundreds of likes and countless shares. People were miserable.

Even the "nice" rejections hurt, often a personalized email with detailed feedback and praise for the manuscript, only to end negatively, the agent or publisher delivering the bad news. Ultimately, nice rejections were more painful. The pang of being so close but sorry, *You're just not good enough*.

By the end of the week, a writer's spreadsheet had more blotted out lines marked REJECTED than it did clear lines. The clear lines meant hope. And yet a writer had started to find the whole process senseless. They felt the urge to move on, abandon the manuscript, and write something new.

Hobbies include: Collecting my rejections, alphabetizing my rejections, talking to my rejections, letting my rejections talk to me.

They counted how many rejections they had: 76. It looked like a fake number. The numbers didn't seem to add up except as confirmation that a writer could write, but it didn't mean they would be published. A writer discovered there was a distinction between writing and publishing. Publishing was a business after all.

Still, a writer couldn't help but feel demoralized.

And then they saw someone else's book deal announcement. A "very nice" deal according to the listing. They had their agent and their auction, bidding war between multiple editors; a writer read the premise of the book three times and found none of it enticing. It sounded like another campus novel, and the title? It was bad. It was one of those "long phrase" titles, clearly inspired by a certain popular Raymond Carver story collection.

They were bitter, and because everyone else on social media was bitter too, their next post went viral.

 Give the writer in your life the gift they REALLY want - a seven-figure book deal.

The post reached 1k likes and 452 shares between the time they signed out and signed back in, effectively about two hours. And it didn't stop until a writer tempted deleting the post.

But they didn't.

Maybe this was the best they could ever do:

Be popular on online. Rejected everywhere else.

Everyone seemed to be doing better than them. A writer spent more time lurking on social media, watching streaming movies, listening to music, anything but going out. Their life became highly predictable: work, home, work, home. Same as their status as a writer: Submit, reject, submit, reject.

For a month or two, they stopped submitting.

A writer posted, deleted posts, and posted again. They developed a list of nemesis accounts, writers that seemed so earnest and "successful" that it made them feel horrible about their own situation. Feeling horrible about their own situation had become the one thing they understood. Anger, resentment—it was so easy to read all the posts about having a productive writing day, sharing tips about self-care, and generally acting like happy people. A writer wasn't happy though. They weren't sure what "happy" even meant, so they developed minor back stories for these accounts. They muted hundreds of people they followed, anyone that wasn't complaining. They had become so sensitive and exhausted. Though they wouldn't stop resenting people online, they started to abandon social media.

The rejections poured in, and the ones that didn't even respond were assumed to be rejections too. They found themselves fleeing reality, becoming a runaway themselves, reading book after book while pretending they were the author of said book.

They fantasized about being a published author.

A successful author.

Even though they hadn't a clue what that meant.

 Performance art where a person sits down, picks up a book, and reads nonstop (up to 25min) without looking at their phone.

And when reading or posting about reading no longer worked—a writer got headaches or fell asleep whenever they stared at the page—they fixated on the literary community. They wanted their approval, craving the attention from the same people they had made into villains.

The ideal literary reading—
- 30 sec intro
- 5-8 min read; well-paced, take your time, don't rush
- "Thank you" & walk off stage

The typical literary reading—
- up to 3 min intro w/ circuitous logic
- ~~like~~ 25 min read, erratic, writer self-conscious
- "uhh" doesn't leave stage

Entrance music for authors at literary readings so that nobody has to ever intro their work ever again.

Person who invented literary readings: *sitting at a bar reading a book* "I wish this was worse."

A writer tempted the role of "literary citizenship" in hopes that their advocacy and encouragement might help their career. By that, a writer meant: land a book deal.

Of course, a writer would find out that care and compassion weren't always reciprocated, and their efforts, though appreciated by some, wouldn't blossom into help when they found themselves in need.

The three stages of literary event excitement:

1) (Puts on calendar) Can't fucking wait.
2) ...
3) (Night of) Eh, I'm happy staying home.

They started to flake on literary events they said they'd attend, battling growing resentment whenever someone they helped and cheered on ended up giving opportunities to other people–the more popular people with book deals who were higher up on the social ladder. The resentment grew, yet what else could a writer do but feel sorry for themselves while posturing sad and sarcastic online? Sometimes it felt good to embrace the sorrow, entertaining those equally miserable with their content, the miserable replying with banter. Their own little pity party.

A writer thought of a comedian, any comedian, and the phrase, "misery loves company." They did not agree, misery loves being left the hell alone to make fun of and slander the company. Every piece of comedy was at the expense of someone or something else.

When we clap at the end of a reading, most of the time we're really clapping because it's over.

They were almost always forgotten and passed over by even their so-called writer-friends. Early in an acquaintanceship, when both sides tend to like each other's posts and comment frequently—using gestures of encouragement and comedic whimsy—the thought of cultivating a friendship was genuine. Maybe it gets to the point where both writers trade work, reading each other's newest pieces, hopeful of their impressions and feedback. But most of the time, the early days, the honeymoon period ends and most of the writers stop liking their posts, a writer noticing a drop-off in engagement. Was it something they said? Maybe something they did? Or the more likely, a writer had worn out the interest. Whenever this happened, a writer couldn't help but feel like the world was out to get them.

At the worst times, they felt invisible.

At the best of times, they gained motivation by being continually underappreciated.

Character so real you think you know them.
Person so fake you think someone made them up.

Writing goals and standards—

I really like writing.
Amended: I kind of like writing.
Amended: I like writing when I'm inspired.
Amended: I tell people I like writing.

Everyone was, indeed, doing better than them. A writer worked on their own platform, imagining it as a literal platform made of material only as solid as their self-worth. This meant thin glass that shattered the moment any weight at all burdened the base. A platform, they mused. What happened to having friends? What happened to being a person rather than a brand? It was all data on a network server, at the end of the day.

A writer no longer wrote or submitted their work. They created a mental list of people they thought hated them, never remembered them, thought of a writer as nothing worth their time. And then they cross-checked it with the people they hated, the nemesis list, and realized so many were one and the same. It didn't feel good at all.

They fixated on reading series, presses, people who ignored them.

In short order, a writer became funnier and snarkier on social media.

 A ghost: Scares the hell out of you.
A zombie: Eats your brains.
A vampire: Sucks the life out of you.
Writing a novel: All of the above.

A writer pinpointed the source of their popularity: They were popular because they were miserable. They were miserable because they were popular for their misery.

 T-shirt: Feed your mind (with books) and then destroy your mind (with booze).

Maybe no one would ever read their writing. A writer learned to mentally prepare themselves for universal rejection.

Friday night for a writer –

Everyone: "I'm going out for drinks with friends; you should come along!"
Writer: *texting from bar, alone* "Naw, I'm writing tonight"

They picked up a new book, something that was sent to them by a publicist working for a mid-sized publisher, ironically one of the presses that recently rejected their manuscript. A writer gave it a few pages, couldn't concentrate on the prose, flipped to the back cover to read all the promotional materials and blurbs. Seeing the phrase "tour-de-force" caused them to toss the galley to the floor where it remained for days. *Fuck you and your "tour-de-force,"* a writer thought. A writer absentmindedly scrolled through social media and eventually lost interest in that too, but not before posting again.

A book a day keeps social interaction away.

A writer might never write again. Rejection was truly debilitating, especially the kind ones. It hurt to see their hard work go unwanted. The rejections slowed down completely, and they hadn't bothered to continue submitting any work.

Their presence had become a charade, all these posts about writing when they no longer cared about writing.

Platform.

Brand.

Following.

The words echoed in a writer's mind.

Their heart wasn't in it and they had begun to reuse old posts: finding the original post, deleting it, and posting it as an original.

No one seemed to notice, which made them feel even worse.

A person only ever had a single moment in the spotlight, and what if a writer had wasted it on social media?

 #WhyIWrite I don't know. Stop asking.

Life went on surprisingly easy. A writer allowed themselves to become consumed with their job. They started hanging out often with a group from work that played a lot of video games and went to a lot of rock concerts. A writer started dabbling with guitar.

They thought about pivoting their energies and enthusiasm to music.

But all it took was checking social media and finding out about a book that was publishing soon, one that sounded eerily like theirs, to be pulled back into writerly despair.

 98% of writing is just tricking yourself psychologically to keep going.

A writer returned to their Excel spreadsheet and counted the number of submissions that had yet to receive a reply. There were four. All of them indie presses. A writer looked at the short list of presses they hadn't tried yet and then submitted to all eight in a single Monday afternoon while at work.

When they checked the masthead of a new publisher they had heard about, publishing a lot of books that seemed fascinating, they noticed they followed each other on social media. Was this enough of a precedent to reach out and see if they wanted to look at their novel?

Writing books is a whole lot like getting a credit card—

There's 0 interest for at least 1 year. By the time the second year rolls around, you've incurred debt that'll take years to pay off.

A writer wasn't sure, but really, what was there to lose? They DMed the editor and immediately signed out for the remainder of the workday.

Writing a book is an endless cycle of confusion, despair, and doubt punctuated by brief yet frequent moments of coffee.

They found it incredibly easy to ignore all the writing/rejection related stuff now that they had their group of friends. They were excited that a band they all liked was coming to town and one of the friends could get free VIP backstage passes to the show.

Novel — "Some crazy shit that didn't happen."
Memoir — "Some crazy shit that happened."
Poetry — "Some crazy shit."

The next time they checked social media, a writer noticed a new DM waiting. Sure enough, the editor had replied. Beyond the pleasantries, the usual chatter about what they were currently reading, thanking a writer for offering such kind words about their publishing house. They gave their email address and encouraged them to send their book.

A writer replied in earnest. They were anxious about how long they should take before sending. *Would it look bad if they sent it immediately?*

They couldn't wait, so within the hour, they sent the full manuscript with their query.

It took Tolkien 16 years to write Lord of the Rings. 2.5 days for Boyne to write the international bestseller, The Boy in the Striped Pajamas. Your pet cat probably just finished writing a novel about addiction and catnip.
Point is—it takes as long as it takes to write a book because every goddamn book is unique.

Some time passed. They couldn't remember how long. Forgetting they ever sent it to the editor was a writer's way of coping with the high likelihood that it would be, once again, a rejection. Still, often they would find themselves dreaming up the acceptance, what it might feel like to see the email in their inbox, waiting in anticipation of saving them from yet another day of waiting. They also wondered what could be taking so long—what do editors do anyway? A writer had seen a thread online claiming editors no longer accepted manuscripts that weren't essentially ready for print, leaving all the editing to the writer and/or the agent. A writer wondered if editors could be lazy too, ignoring their stack of manuscripts and binging some new show. Maybe an editor could be hungover somewhere, neglecting their job in the face of courting new addictions. Or it could be none of that—an editor didn't like the book and was kicking the rejection email down the line, waiting as long as they could before having to send it, because it probably made an editor feel bad too. The worst of all possibilities.

Eventually, they entertained new ideas for novels. It was all they had to keep motivated.

 After writing has become a habit, only then will you achieve something. By then, you'll be too busy feeding the habit to actually enjoy it.

A writer needed a new project to feel whole. They filled a notebook with various notes and concepts for their second novel.

It became a morning ritual. Writing in their notebook reminded them why they loved to write, why they bothered at all.

Remember why we started writing in the first place: for ourselves.

A writer got an email from the editor.

It arrived on a Wednesday afternoon while they were at work.

The subject line was, "Your Manuscript." The body of the email was simple, "Hey, I finished reading your book! Do you have time to chat about it over the phone sometime today?"

A writer cleared everything and ran into a nearby conference room to take the call.

They reread the email a dozen times, worrying that the editor might be like, "It's good but needs a lot of work," or something placating like that to essentially hide the fact that it's a rejection."

Started writing to work through PTSD / develops PTSD because started writing.

A writer emailed back, "Free whenever!" Probably too eager, sounding quite desperate, but at this point, a writer didn't care.

Life stages of a manuscript:

Birth (first draft) - It's not done yet.
Adolescence (fifteenth draft) - It's not done yet.
Adulthood (final draft) - It's not done yet.
Old age (publication) – I guess it's done?

They just wanted to get it over with. The editor was free in an hour, but they still moved into the conference room, booking it as a business call, and ignored their to-do list of tasks. Instead, they scrolled through the press website, reading about the history of the house, checking out their upcoming titles, and eventually moved to YouTube to watch video interviews of the editor and anything involving the press.

 Author: "Publish my book."
Publisher: "Okay."
Dramatization: Not at all how the publishing process works.

A writer lost interest in social media. The latest post had all the makings of becoming another trending post, yet their interest wandered. They daydreamed about how the call might play out. And then there it was, a new number, New York City area code.

They answered.

 Writer after writing anything: "I'm at my creative peak and can die happy."
Writer 10 minutes later: "I'm all out of ideas and I'm going to die alone."

The call went extremely well. One of the first things out of the editor's mouth was that they loved the book and wanted to publish it. A writer was so giddy they could barely speak. The call lasted about thirty minutes. The editor talked about the publishing timeline for the the book. It would be two years before it would make it to store shelves, which was a little alarming, but a writer didn't care: They were going to be published!

> If there is one thing about writing books that I have learned, it's that I haven't learned anything about writing books.

After the call, they sat in the conference room for a while, musing about their path to publication. It hadn't gone as they planned. Countless rejections, doubt, and several moments where they actually wanted to quit writing.

But now they had "made it."

A book of theirs would someday exist.

It fueled their next novel, the enthusiasm for the great unknown, the fact that they would have one book suddenly grew to include the thought that they might be able to publish a second book.

> The main thing is — begin writing your novel heartfelt and make sure to end it heartbroken.

A writer was equally excited and overwhelmed by the thought of starting over, writing a new book. They cherished that hopeful notebook filled with ideas.

> Up, Up, Down, Down, Left, Right, Left, Right, B, A, Start Over Your Novel

The video game sessions with their work office buds soon became a thing of the past. Their weekends became writing marathons, and yet again, their social life suffered. But they were a writer. This is what they did. And they wouldn't want to do anything else.

 To write something, you learn to live in it; to finish something, you learn to let it go.

A writer received invitations to read at various reading series around town and even ones in L.A., N.Y.C., and Chicago. They were invited to speak to the editor's friend's class, the friend being a fellow press-mate.

They were, at first, excited and then nervous about all of it.

People wanted to hear about what they had learned about the craft of writing. It was an amazing thing to behold. They tried their hardest to enjoy what was happening and to silence all negative thoughts. Their Imposter Syndrome could kick in at any moment and they wanted to enjoy this.

In their lecture, they defined this feeling of contentment and, surprisingly, a genuine surge of happiness that came not from the publication of the book, but rather the realization that they had completed it—they had written a book that others read. Maybe not millions, but some. Some people enjoyed their book.

A writer didn't want this to run away.

Runaway –

(n) An idea, story, or mood that escapes you the moment you are right in the middle of experiencing it.

They thought about posting the definition of *runaway*, but then stopped short. Why bother? A writer would get to interact with people face-to-face, writers both experienced and aspiring.

When they signed back into their account, they checked and saw that it had been over a week since their last post. Yet they couldn't gather up the energy or creativity to post something new.

They would have to relearn how to write.

It would never get any easier, and that was okay.

> Life lessons you can learn from writers –
>
>
>
> • Coffee is a food group
> • Take more naps
> • Just one more YouTube video
> • Rules were made to be broken (so are deadlines)
> • Find joy in the simple (meaning FREE) things
> • Go towards fear, it'll make for a better story

A writer booked their flight, discovered that the university would pay for their hotel and provide a meal stipend. They planned on it being, altogether, a four-day trip. They received edits from their editor a day before the flight. They were eight days into the writing of the first draft of their second novel. Excited about everything, a writer tempted telling their editor about the new book. But they didn't—it was too early. They wanted to live in it a little bit longer.

> To write, you learn to focus, sacrifice time, and be alone with your thoughts.
> To edit, you learn to collaborate with others.
> To publish, you learn to process feedback.
> To promote, you relearn what it takes to be human (i.e. manage anxieties).

A writer didn't want it all to run away from them too quickly. It would get its chance later. For the moment, they wanted to hold onto it. For as long as they could. Hold on. They held on.

> Author's last words —
>
> "I want nothing but death."—Jane Austen
> "I love many things. I love all people."—Tolstoy
> "I must go in; the fog is rising."—Emily Dickinson
> "Kill me! Or you are a murderer!" —Kafka
> "Does nobody understand?"—James Joyce
> "I don't think they even heard me."—Yukio Mishima
> "Will this book be enough?"—Me

Author bios are seldom brutally honest. My question is, why not? An author's bio should reveal the full scope of their situation, as of the current printing.

@mjseidlinger is the recipient of 140k in student loan debt and currently has $210.68 in his checking account. He spends most of his time trying to make rent while trying to cultivate sustainable hobbies to keep his mental health stable. You better believe he's working on a novel.

FUTURETENSEBOOKS.COM

CPSIA information can be obtained
at www.ICGtesting.com
Printed in the USA
BVHW030727210921
617107BV00004B/15